Dear Parents and Educators,

Welcome to Penguin Young Readers! As parents and educators, you know that each child develops at his or her own pace—in terms of speech, critical thinking, and, of course, reading. Penguin Young Readers recognizes this fact. As a result, each Penguin Young Readers book is assigned a traditional easy-to-read level (1–4) as well as a Guided Reading Level (A–P). Both of these systems will help you choose the right book for your child. Please refer to the back of each book for specific leveling information. Penguin Young Readers features esteemed authors and illustrators, stories about favorite characters, fascinating nonfiction, and more!

Corduroy Writes a Letter

LEVEL 2

GUIDED READING LEVEL **I**

This book is perfect for a **Progressing Reader** who:
- can figure out unknown words by using picture and context clues;
- can recognize beginning, middle, and ending sounds;
- can make and confirm predictions about what will happen in the text; and
- can distinguish between fiction and nonfiction.

Here are some **activities** you can do during and after reading this book:
- Picture Clues: Picture clues help young readers figure out the meaning of words. Read this book and have the child point to the pictures and the corresponding words.
- Sight Words: Sight words are frequently used words that readers must know just by looking at them. They are known instantly, on sight. Knowing these words helps children develop into efficient readers. As you read the story, have the child point out the sight words below.

after	every	going	know	then
ask	from	just	put	were

Remember, sharing the love of reading with a child is the best gift you can give!

—Sarah Fabiny, Editorial Director
    Penguin Young Readers program

*Penguin Young Readers are leveled by independent reviewers applying the standards developed by Irene Fountas and Gay Su Pinnell in *Matching Books to Readers: Using Leveled Books in Guided Reading*, Heinemann, 1999.

PENGUIN YOUNG READERS
An Imprint of Penguin Random House LLC

The Library of Congress has catalogued the Viking edition
under the following Control Number: 2002006154

ISBN 9781524788650 (pbk)   10 9 8 7 6 5 4
ISBN 9781524788667 (hc)   10 9 8 7 6 5 4 3 2

CORDUROY
Writes a Letter

by Alison Inches
illustrated by Allan Eitzen
based on the characters created by Don Freeman

Penguin Young Readers
An Imprint of Penguin Random House

Lisa took a big bite out of

her cookie.

"Something's different.

I know what it is.

It doesn't have enough sprinkles!"

"Why don't you write a letter to the bakery?" said her mother.

"Good idea!" said Lisa.

She got out a pen and a pad of paper.

She stared at the pad.

The clock went

Tick tick.

Tick tick.

After a while, she said,

"What's the use, Corduroy?

The baker will not listen to me.

I'm just a little girl."

She put down her pen and left.

Maybe I can write a letter, thought

Corduroy.

Dear Mr. Baker:

We love your cookies.

We buy them every week.

Today there were fewer sprinkles.

We thought you should know.

From,

Corduroy

Corduroy put the letter

in the mailbox.

The next week, Lisa and Corduroy picked up the cookies.

"Look, Corduroy!" said Lisa.

"The cookies have more sprinkles!"

"That's right!" said the baker.

"Someone sent me a letter."

THEATER

That night, Lisa and her mother
went to the movies.

Corduroy went, too.

"Hey, look at the sign!" said Lisa.

"The lights are out on two of
the letters."

"Why don't you write the owner
a letter?" said her mother.

"Maybe I will," said Lisa.

15

Later, Lisa got a pen and a pad
of paper.

"What should I write, Corduroy?"
asked Lisa.

Soon she began to feel sleepy.

"It's no use," said Lisa.

"The movie theater owner is
too important.

He will not read a letter from me."

She went to bed.

But Corduroy was not
ready for bed.

I can write a letter, he thought.

THEATER

A few days later, Lisa and her mother walked past the movie theater.

Lisa looked at the sign.

"It's all fixed!" she said.

"That's neat," said Lisa.

"The next time I have something
to say, I'm going to
write a letter."

Every day, Lisa listened to music on the radio.

Corduroy listened, too.

"I love this new radio station," said Lisa.

"But I wish they would play the
song 'Teddy Bear Bop.'
I should write to the station
and ask them to play it," said Lisa.
Great idea! thought Corduroy.

Lisa got her pen and pad.

She wrote:

Dear WROC:

I listen to your station every day.

I wish you would play

"Teddy Bear Bop."

I love that song.

My bear Corduroy loves it, too.

Thanks for being

the best station ever.

Yours truly,

Lisa

Lisa put the letter

in the mailbox.

The next week,

Lisa had the radio on.

The person on the radio
said, "This next song is for
Corduroy from Lisa."
Then "Teddy Bear Bop"
began to play.
Lisa and Corduroy danced
around the room.

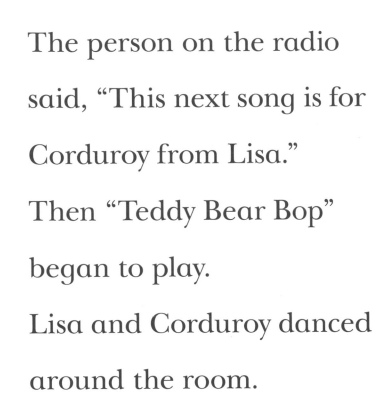

"Wow!" said Lisa.

"They're playing our song!"

See, thought Corduroy.

It pays to write letters!